FOR
ANNA-BIRGITTE

Text, cover, illustrations, and book design by Stian Hole

© 2013 Cappelen Damm
Originally published in Norwegian under the title
Annas himmel
This English language translation © Don Bartlett

Published in 2014 by Eerdmans Books for Young Readers,
an imprint of Wm. B. Eerdmans Publishing Co.
2140 Oak Industrial Dr. NE
Grand Rapids, Michigan 49505
P.O. Box 163, Cambridge CB3 9PU U.K.

www.eerdmans.com/youngreaders

Manufactured at Tien Wah Press
in Malaysia in March 2014, first printing

19 18 17 16 15 14   9 8 7 6 5 4 3 2 1

Thanks to Ellen Seip and John Erik Riley.
Published with support from the Norwegian Cultural Fund.

Library of Congress Cataloging-in-Publication Data

Hole, Stian, author, illustrator.
[Annas Himmel. English.]
Anna's heaven / written and illustrated by Stian Hole ;
translated by Don Bartlett.
pages cm
Summary: After the death of her mother, Anna and her
father imagine that Heaven might be a place where
one can help in God's garden, visit with old friends,
and take off one's socks whenever one pleases.
ISBN 978-0-8028-5441-4
[1. Heaven — Fiction. 2. Future life — Fiction. 3. Fathers
and daughters — Fiction. 4. Death — Fiction.
5. Imagination — Fiction.] I. Bartlett, Don. II. Title.
PZ7.H7072Ann 2014
[Fic] — dc23
2013044518

This translation has been published
with the financial support of NORLA.

Stian Hole
Anna's Heaven

EERDMANS BOOKS FOR YOUNG READERS

GRAND RAPIDS, MICHIGAN • CAMBRIDGE, U.K.

"You can spell *kayak* forward or backward and it's the same word," Anna says. "Like *redder*."

"And *Anna*," Dad says. "Hurry up now or we'll be late."

Even though she is looking away, Anna notices that her father is restless. She can feel it in the air, in the grass, in the scar on her knee, in the mole on her neck, and in every hair on her head. Anna knows that her dad gets restless when he is not looking forward to something.

"There must be something in the air, because my hair is full of static," Anna says, gazing up at the sky. "The clouds are in a hurry, just like you. When I close my eyes, I can see whatever I want."

"Hurry up, Anna," her father says. At that moment they hear the church bells chime from across the fjord.

Anna has all the time in the world.
"Look, Dad, the coffee pot and the elephant
are from the same family!" she says.

But he doesn't answer.

Mom said birds were flowers that could fly, and that the sunflower was the sun's little sister," Anna says. "Look! Swallows are writing cursive letters in the sky. Maybe they're making shopping lists for us. And a recipe for strawberry tart." Anna follows two swallows with her fingers.

"oday there's someone in the sky sending down nails. That's not right, is it?" Dad says.

"No," Anna whispers, "but tomorrow there might be strawberries with honey."

"**H**ow can God keep his eye on everyone?" Anna asks.

Dad shrugs his shoulders.

"Was God better in the old days?" Anna scratches the mosquito bite on her calf.

"I don't know, Anna."

"Perhaps God's beginning to get forgetful like Grandma," Anna says.

AIR MAIL

"**W**hy can't he who knows everything, who can pull and push and turn over clouds and waves and planets — why can't he invent something to turn bad into good?" Anna says.

"God should hang up a mailbox for people to send questions and complaints," Dad answers.

"**I**f only Mom could come back and braid my hair,"
Anna sighs.

"Ah, if only she could," Dad says.

"One day while Mom was brushing her hair in front
of the mirror, she said everything had two sides."
Anna gives that some thought. "Do you think
there's anything on the other side of the mirror?"

"I don't know, Anna, my sweet," Dad says,
squeezing his eyes shut.

"Look, Dad! There's a hole in the sky. Come on, let's jump!"

"Where are we going, Anna?"

"Far away, Dad. We're going to swim to the Mariana Trench, and then we'll fly through the Crab Nebula to a place where the sky is under water."

"Oh, right," Dad says, but he doesn't really understand. He hesitates, but then he jumps after her.

"**W**e'll follow the flying fish. They must know the way," Anna says.

"**L**isten! The sea has so many voices," Anna whispers. "It sounds like a heavenly choir humming. A song about crabs, eels, and sea urchins cooing in the deep."

"Can you fish for mackerel in heaven?" Anna asks. "And sleep in on Sundays?"

"I think you can take your socks off whenever you please, at any rate," Dad answers.

"Like the President of the United States does," Anna says.

"If you've got to look after everyone, you must have more arms than an octopus — and longer ones, too," she adds.

"**H**ere are all the people we can't see, Dad. Grandad is down to the left of the lighthouse, rocking in his chair as always. There. I can see the old postman. Mom said he read people's letters," Anna says.

"**N**ow and then some letters do disappear along the way," Dad answers.

"I can't see Mom anywhere," Anna says. "Perhaps she's in Paradise, doing some weeding. God would be pleased to have a gardener. He might need a hand with the garden if he's got so much else on his mind."

"**O**r she's visiting someone she hasn't seen for a while," Anna says. "I bet she's wearing her new dress, the one from Spain."

"**M**om might have gone to the library," Anna suggests.

"Does God read books?" Dad exclaims in surprise.

"Of course he does. He's got a big library. Even God needs an encyclopedia to look things up now and then."

"It can't be easy for him to remember everything," Dad says.

"These are places I've never been before," Dad says. "I'm glad you brought me. But how do we get home?"

"We'll do what cats do when they fall from the ninth floor — twirl around and land on our feet!" Anna answers.

At last, Dad smiles.

"**N**ow I'm ready. Hurry up, Dad. We've got to go or we'll be late."